# ZAPATO POWER
# FREDDIE RAMOS RULES NEW YORK

JACQUELINE JULES    art by MIGUEL BENÍTEZ

albert Whitman & Company
Chicago, Illinois

Don't miss the first five **zapato power** books!

# Freddie Ramos Takes Off
# Freddie Ramos Springs into Action
# Freddie Ramos Zooms to the Rescue
# Freddie Ramos Makes a Splash
# Freddie Ramos Stomps the Snow
# Freddie Ramos Hears It All
# Freddie Ramos Adds It All Up

Library of Congress Cataloging-in-Publication Data
Jules, Jacqueline.| Benítez, Miguel, illustrator.
Freddie Ramos rules New York /
Jacqueline Jules ; art by Miguel Benítez.
Chicago, Illinois : Albert Whitman & Company, 2016.
Series: Zapato power ; 6
Summary: On a visit to New York City to see Uncle Jorge,
Freddie brings his new sneakers; his old sneakers gave him super speed
but were becoming too small for his growing feet.
Subjects: | CYAC: Sneakers—Fiction. | Inventions—Fiction. |
Hispanic Americans—Fiction. | New York (N.Y.)—Fiction. |
BISAC: JUVENILE FICTION / People & Places / United States /
Hispanic & Latino. | JUVENILE FICTION / Action & Adventure / General. |
JUVENILE FICTION / Readers / Chapter Books.
Classification: LCC PZ7.J92947 Fo 2016
DDC [Fic]—dc23
LC record available at https://lccn.loc.gov/2016041989

Printed in the United States of America
10  9  8  7  6  5  4  3  2  LB  24  23  22  21  20  19

For more information about Albert Whitman & Company,
visit our website at www.albertwhitman.com.

**For Neal**
**Your spirit lives on in New York City.**

# CONTENTS

# 1. Ready for New York

I was all dressed for my trip to New York. Except for my sneakers. Getting my feet into my purple zapatos took extra time. First, I had to put on band-aids to cover my blisters. Then I had to push and pull and stomp.

Mom watched me from the doorway of my room.

"Freddie?" she asked. "Are your sneakers too tight?"

That was not a question I wanted to answer. My feet had gotten bigger. But the last thing I wanted was a new pair of shoes. The ones I had were special. They gave me super speed and super bounce. I couldn't give them up.

"New York City has great stores," Mom said. "We can buy new shoes on our trip to see Uncle Jorge."

"That's okay, Mom," I said, stomping each foot again. "These are fine."

"I'm not so sure." Mom folded her arms and frowned.

"We can worry about my shoes when we get home," I answered. "In New York, I want to see the things Uncle Jorge told us about on the phone. The huge Christmas tree at Rockefeller Center and the lights of Times Square."

"*Yo también.*" Mom smiled. "Are you ready?"

"Almost. Can I say good-bye to my friends?"

Mom held up one finger. "We're leaving in an hour."

"I'll be fast."

# ZOOM! ZOOM! ZAPATO!

With my super zapatos, I could leave 29G and go clear across Starwood Park Apartments in a blink.

"Mr. Vaslov!" I knocked on his toolshed. "It's Freddie!"

No answer. That wasn't strange.
Mr. Vaslov takes care of Starwood
Park. He was always out fixing
leaky sinks and broken toilets.
I just felt sad about going to New
York without saying good-bye.
Mr. Vaslov had changed my life. He
invented sneakers with super speed
and gave them to me to test out.

# ZOOM! ZOOM! ZaPaTO!

I left the toolshed and zoomed
back to 28G, where Maria and her
little brother, Gio, live. They were
our neighbors, and they had our

key to 29G so they could feed my
guinea pig while we were away.
I trusted Maria, but I needed to
remind Gio about a few things.

"Don't let Claude the Second out
of his cage," I told Gio. "He'll leave
poop presents on the carpet."

"I won't," Gio promised.

"And don't forget to give
him a carrot every day," I
added.

"Don't worry, Freddie,"
Maria said. "We can
take care of your
guinea pig for
three days."

Three days. This was my first trip to New York. Every other time I'd seen my Uncle Jorge, he had come to visit us.

"Are you going to see a parade with big balloons?" Gio asked. "Like I saw on TV?"

"No," I answered. "That was last month, at Thanksgiving time."

"Then why are you going?" Gio asked.

"Mom said Uncle Jorge is planning something special."

"What?"

I shrugged my shoulders. "Mom said she couldn't tell me yet."

"Is it a secret?"

Gio asks too many questions, but not all of them are bad. I headed home to get some answers.

## 2. A Present

When I opened the door to 29G, Mr. Vaslov was in my living room talking to Mom. I was going to get a chance to say good-bye after all!

"Can you deliver this for me?" Mr. Vaslov handed Mom a white envelope with an address printed in black letters. "My brother needs these papers tomorrow."

"The zip code is the same as Jorge's," Mom said. "It should be nearby."

"Thank you," Mr. Vaslov said. "This is important to my family."

He nodded his bushy gray head and turned around. That's when he noticed me.

"Freddie!" His face broke into a big smile. "I have a present for you."

Mr. Vaslov picked up a wrapped box. I held my breath. The last time Mr. Vaslov gave me a gift, it

was my sneakers with super speed. I
wondered what would happen now.

"Open it!" Mr. Vaslov said.

I sat down on the couch and
ripped off the red-and-green
wrapping paper.

"New sneakers!" Mom clapped.
"Mr. Vaslov! This is too generous!"

"Freddie helps me around
Starwood Park," Mr. Vaslov told
Mom. "Think of this as a thank-
you."

"They look just like my old ones!"
I held them up. They had the same
purple color with silver wings on
the sides. "Only bigger! How did you

know my old shoes were tight?" I hadn't told anyone before today, not even my guinea pig.

Mr. Vaslov laughed. "You've been growing, Freddie, like all healthy kids."

I guess some things are not easy to hide.

"Put them on, Freddie," Mom suggested. "You can wear them to New York."

My new zapatos slipped on easily. There was no need to stuff in my feet. But comfy toes weren't better than super speed. I headed outside for a test run.

"Where are you going, Freddie?" Mom stopped me. "We have to leave for the bus."

I felt trapped. Our apartment had too many walls for zooming ninety miles an hour. I looked at Mr. Vaslov for help. He was bending down to pick up my old shoes, the ones that were too small.

"I'd like to take these with me." He put them into the box.

"Of course," Mom said. "Maybe you know of another little boy who can use them."

My heart thumped in my chest. Was Mr. Vaslov going to give

someone else at Starwood Park my special sneakers? Who?

Super speed is a big responsibility. And it's not easy to control. I had trouble before Mr. Vaslov invented a Zapato Power wristband with on and off buttons.

"Have a good trip!" Mr. Vaslov waved good-bye at my front door.

"Don't go!" I tugged on his arm.

"What is it, Freddie?" Mr. Vaslov glanced over at Mom to remind me she was in the room.

"Uh…" My tongue felt dry. Mr. Vaslov and I didn't talk about Zapato Power in front of her. Moms

get scared at the thought of kids
running ninety miles an hour and
bouncing twenty feet in the air. A
good superhero doesn't make his
mom worry.

"Thank you for the shoes," I
sputtered.

Mr. Vaslov winked. "I hope they work well for you."

I did too. Was Mr. Vaslov not sure? Some of his inventions didn't do what he expected. At least not at first. What if my new shoes didn't give me super speed?

"Freddie!" Mom put Mr. Vaslov's white envelope into her purse and grabbed the handle of our rolling suitcase. "*¡Vamos!*"

I stepped outside, sticking close to Mr. Vaslov, hoping we could talk alone while Mom locked the door. But his phone rang in his pocket.

"Dripping faucet?" he repeated. "In 35D? I'll be right there."

Mr. Vaslov hurried off to get his tools, leaving me with a head full of questions.

What was in the white envelope? Who was getting my too-small zapatos? Would my new purple sneakers be as fast as my old ones? And what was Uncle Jorge's surprise?

## 3. The Lady with the Earbuds

The bus to New York was big. And it was bright orange. I felt like I was walking into a giant pumpkin.

"Take the window seat, Freddie," Mom said. "You'll have fun looking out."

All I could see was brown fields, old buildings, and a few cows here and there. And all I could think about was running. Were my new zapatos as fast as my old ones? Could I zoom along the side of the road and beat the bus? Or outrun the cows if they chased me?

"Try to sit still, Freddie." Mom touched my knee.

Being on the bus was like being in school too long without a playground break. My legs got squirmy.

"Don't kick the back of my seat!" A blond lady wearing earbuds turned to yell at me.

"Sorry!" I hugged my legs against my chest.

"Be patient, Freddie," Mom
said. "New York will be worth the
wait."

I hoped so. And I hoped I could
use Zapato Power there—and that

running superfast wouldn't get me super lost in a big city.

Mom handed me a book. The moving bus made the words jump. That left me looking out the window again. I rubbed the buttons on my wristband and pretended I was outside, running to New York with my super zapatos.

A few seconds later, I heard a man's voice.

*"Eduardo kissed Vivian on her soft red lips."*

Who was talking mushy stuff? On a bus?

I popped my head over the headrest. The blond lady with the earbuds was holding a book in her hands.

*"Vivian, you are the love of my life."*

I turned to the seat behind me. A little boy had his hand in a bag of cheese puffs. His cheeks looked too orange to be talking in a deep voice to someone named Vivian.

*"She closed her dreamy blue eyes."*

Yuck! Mom wouldn't want me hearing this! Why wasn't she covering my ears? Because she was asleep! The noise wasn't bothering her at all.

*"Eduardo! Run away with me tonight."*

I looked all around the bus. The sound wasn't coming from the side or the back. It was coming from the blond lady's earbuds! How come I could hear it?

I stared at my Zapato Power wristband. It was warm. I rubbed the buttons a little. The wristband cooled down and the mushy voices stopped.

Uh-oh! Did my new zapatos give me super hearing? What about super speed? And super bounce? Could they do all three? I had two buttons on my wristband. What if two powers was all I got? Which ones did I want the most?

Super hearing would be good when I wanted to hear what grown-ups were saying. Would I like it as much as running fast?

I had to get off the bus and find out what my new shoes could do! But I was stuck in the window seat, watching more brown fields and buildings go by. How much longer till New York?

Just when I thought I couldn't wait another second, I heard another sound. This time, it was something everybody on the bus heard, not just the lady with earbuds and the boy with Zapato Power.

**Bang! Bumpity! Bumpity! Bump! Bump!**

Mom sat straight up. "What was that?"

The driver pulled over beside an open field and told us to get out. We had a flat tire.

"*Mala suerte*," Mom complained.

It was bad luck for Mom and lots of grumpy-faced people getting off the bus. Not for me! I could finally test my new sneakers.

# ZOOM! ZOOM! ZAPATO!

I circled the field three times.
Just like always, Zapato Power
smoke whooshed out of my heels.
It covered me in a cloud, making
me invisible. No one, not even my
mom, noticed me disappear and
come back in a blink.

## ZOOM! ZOOM! ZAPATO!

*¡Fantástico!* I still had super
speed!

# 4. Times Square

The flat tire made us late. By the time we arrived in New York, it was dark and chilly outside. Uncle Jorge said that was okay.

"Times Square looks better at night! You'll love it!"

Uncle Jorge led us through the busy streets to a place full of bright neon signs. Everywhere I looked, I saw a gigantic picture. One of them had a lady with a green face and a pointed black hat.

"Do you have a wicked witch in New York?" I asked Uncle Jorge.

"*Wicked* is a Broadway show, Freddie," Uncle Jorge explained. "A play with singing and dancing."

New York had a lot to get used to. Singing green witches. Tall buildings everywhere. And more people packed together in one place than I'd ever seen.

"Hold on to me, Freddie," Mom kept saying.

Mom squeezed my hand like she thought I could jump over everyone's heads with Zapato Power. I didn't even know if that was true. When the bus stopped for the flat tire, I'd been so busy testing my super speed, I'd forgotten to see if I still had super bounce.

"This way!" Uncle Jorge waved a gloved hand at us.

It wasn't always easy to follow him in the crowd. Luckily, Uncle Jorge was wearing a funky hat with lots of colorful stripes and a row of short strings sticking up. It made him look a little like a rooster. Whenever we got too far apart, I looked for that hat.

Ten minutes later, we turned the corner to a quieter street. Mom finally let go of my hand. I shook it out a little to make sure it wasn't broken.

We crossed an intersection and stepped onto the curb behind an old man with a cane. He was carrying a large brown envelope. A sudden gust of wind blew it out of his hand and down the street.

"*¡Ayúdame!* Help me!" the old man cried.

Uncle Jorge rushed to help, but the wind snatched the envelope away. New York was big and crowded, but it needed Zapato Power just like Starwood Park. I pressed the first button on my wristband.

## ZOOM! ZOOM! ZAPATO!

In a blink, I had the envelope for the old man.

"*¡Gracias! ¡Gracias!*" he exclaimed. "These papers are for my green card."

I knew what a green card was. It was important if you came from another country and wanted to stay in the United States. When someone at Starwood Park got a green card, they invited the neighbors to a party.

"*De nada,*" I said. "No problem."

The old man hugged me and

my chest filled up like a balloon. Helping people was the best part of Zapato Power! I was so glad my new shoes worked!

"That was amazing," Mom said. "I didn't know you could run so fast."

"You're like lightning," Uncle Jorge added.

For a split second, I worried my mom had somehow figured out I had super speed. But her face wasn't scrunched up, like it gets when she thinks I'm going to hurt myself. She was smiling, proud of me.

"You have a good heart, *mi hijo*." We waved good-bye to the old man with the cane and walked a few more blocks to Uncle Jorge's apartment.

"This is where I live." Uncle Jorge pointed to a sand-colored building. "Before we go in, I'd like to go next door."

"Why?" I asked.

"You'll see." Uncle Jorge smiled bigger than a cartoon cat.

We followed him into a bodega store with fruits, vegetables, and other foods. A dark-haired girl stood behind the register. She was taller than me, about middle school size.

Uncle Jorge introduced us. "This is Juanita, the daughter of a very special lady I want you to meet."

"Mamá isn't here," Juanita explained. "She went home to make *pollo asado* for dinner tonight."

"That's my Angela!" Uncle Jorge clapped like he'd won the lottery.

"How nice!" Mom clapped too. "I can't wait to meet her."

A funny feeling came over me. Mom and Uncle Jorge were way too excited about a chicken dinner, even if they were hungry. Something was happening. Something no one had told me yet.

## 5. Uncle Jorge's Secret

We had to go up five flights to my uncle's apartment.

"Sorry, folks," Uncle Jorge said. "There's no elevator."

# ZOOM! ZOOM! Zapato!

All those stairs were asking for Zapato Power. I try to save my shoes

for superhero jobs but sometimes I
can't resist.

Uncle Jorge's apartment had two
bedrooms. He put our suitcase in
the first one where there was a
single bed for Mom and a sleeping
bag for me. It had pink butterflies.

"I borrowed it from Juanita,"
Uncle Jorge said.

While I was looking over my
pink sleeping bag, Mom pulled
Uncle Jorge out into the hallway
and whispered something I
couldn't make out.
Could I hear
what Mom

and Uncle Jorge were saying if I rubbed the buttons on my wristband? Before I could try, the doorbell rang.

"That's Angela!" Uncle Jorge grinned. He opened the front door and a woman with dark hair, who looked a lot like Juanita, walked in. She was carrying a large covered tray that smelled delicious.

"I hope you're hungry!" Angela said.

Right away, I noticed that Angela had dimples in her cheeks, making her smile look extra happy.

Juanita came into the apartment

carrying a smaller tray. She put it
down on the table and whipped
off the foil like a magician doing a
scarf trick.

"*Arroz con leche*," she said. "My
favorite dessert!"

"Mine too!" I said.

"And mine." Uncle Jorge kissed

Angela on the cheek. "You're as sweet as your rice pudding."

The way Uncle Jorge was acting reminded me of the mushy story coming out of the blond lady's earbuds on the bus.

I looked over at Juanita to see how she felt about this. She kept smiling like it was no big deal that Uncle Jorge kissed her mother. I wondered what it would be like if my mom had a special friend. Sometimes it was lonely with just the two of us. Dad was a soldier and a hero. We both missed him a lot.

"*Tengo hambre*," Juanita said, sitting down at the table first.

I was hungry too. I stuffed myself with chicken, beans, and rice pudding. Everybody did. Then we leaned back in our chairs to talk about the next day.

"I'm sorry," Uncle Jorge said. "I have to work."

Uncle Jorge was a manager at a restaurant. Angela owned the bodega next door, and she had to work too.

"Juanita is on winter vacation, just like Freddie," Angela said. "She will take you sightseeing."

"¡*Excelente!*" Mom said. "Only
first we need to deliver something
for a friend from Starwood Park."

Mom got Mr. Vaslov's white
envelope out of her purse. She
showed the address to Juanita.
"Can you find this apartment?"

Juanita nodded. "*Sí.* We can stop
by on our way."

Mom put the envelope on a table
by the front door. "Let's not forget
in the morning."

When Juanita and Angela went
home, Mom sent me to bed. I
wasn't used to sleeping on the floor
in a pink bag. And I wasn't tired.

Besides, there were voices outside my room keeping me up—Mom's voice and Uncle Jorge's voice. They were whispering again. I got out of my sleeping bag and rubbed the buttons on my purple wristband until they got warm. It was like turning up the volume control on the TV. I could hear everything through the door.

"I'm nervous," Uncle Jorge said.

"You'll be fine," Mom said.

"I can't express my feelings," Uncle Jorge said. "I get tongue-tied."

"Write her a letter," Mom suggested.

"*¡Buena idea!*" Uncle Jorge snapped his fingers. "And I'll put the ring inside."

"You won't have to say a word." Mom laughed.

I turned off my Zapato Power hearing. There was no need to listen anymore. I knew what was going on. Uncle Jorge was going to ask Angela to marry him. I was going to have a new aunt and a new cousin!

# 6. The White Envelope

The next morning, Uncle Jorge was whistling. Instead of pouring milk on his cereal, he spilled it on the table. We grabbed paper towels to mop it up.

"My mind is out the window this morning!" Uncle Jorge laughed at himself.

Just as we finished cleaning, the doorbell rang.

"That must be Juanita," Mom said, grabbing my arm. "Let's not keep her waiting."

Mom was in a big hurry to get going. We were all the way down the steps when she realized she'd forgotten Mr. Vaslov's letter.

"*No hay problema*," I told Mom. "I'll be back in a minute."

# ZOOM! ZOOM! ZAPATO!

Uncle Jorge was still whistling when he opened the door.

"What did you forget, Freddie?"

I told him about Mr. Vaslov's envelope. He picked it up off the front table and read the address.

"I can deliver this on my way to work," he said, putting it beside another white envelope inside the front pocket of his jacket.

"Are you sure?" I asked.

Between the whistling and the spilled milk, I wasn't 100 percent positive Uncle Jorge should be trusted with an important letter.

"Of course!" He waved me off. "Go have fun!"

**ZOOM! ZOOM! ZAPATO!**

I dashed back down the steps for a busy morning in New York City.

The first place Juanita took us was Rockefeller Center. It had an ice rink, flags, a gold statue, and a ginormous Christmas tree. Everything in New York was huge!

"We'll come back here tonight," Mom said, "to see the lights on the tree."

In the meantime, we went inside Rockefeller Center to see the city from seventy floors above ground.

"Freddie!" Mom pointed. "Look at the Empire State Building!"

"Which one is it?" I asked.

"The tall one," Mom said. "Can't you see it?"

New York was full of tall buildings. My teacher would say Mom needed to do a better job with description.

"Look over there, Freddie."

Juanita touched my shoulder. "The tallest one with a needle on top."

"I see it now!" I said. "It looks like a giant rocket!"

"You're right!" Juanita agreed.

Some of the buildings had flat tops. Others had round ones. There was a lot to look at. But after a while, my stomach complained for lunch.

Juanita giggled. "Sounds like Freddie needs some New York pizza."

She took us to a place that had the biggest pizza slices I'd ever seen.

"Use two hands, Freddie," Juanita warned me.

It was good advice I should have listened to. Mom had to get a pile of napkins to clean pizza off my jeans. On the bright side, Juanita didn't say, "I told you so." She even gave me her second slice.

"I'm full," Juanita said, passing her paper plate across the table.

"Are you sure?"

She patted her stomach. "Absolutely."

"Thanks!" I smiled at my almost cousin.

Juanita was super nice. It was going to be fun to have a bigger family when Uncle Jorge and Angela got married.

After lunch, Juanita took us to Macy's, this giant department store with more ladies' purses and shoes than I ever wanted to see in one place. Mom loved it! I thought we were going to be stuck there forever.

Then Mom's phone rang.

"What?" she shouted. "You lost the ring? Oh, Jorge!"

Juanita's brown eyes got bigger and bigger as she listened to Mom yell into her phone.

"My mother wanted a diamond from Jorge," Juanita said quietly. "I hope you can find it."

"Don't worry," Mom said. "We will."

But her face didn't look so sure. And I didn't feel so sure I was going to have a bigger family anymore.

# 7. Traffic Jam

We met Uncle Jorge in his office at
the restaurant. He showed us the
letter we were supposed to deliver
for Mr. Vaslov. Uncle Jorge had put
it in his coat pocket beside another
white envelope that morning.

"I wrote out my feelings in a
letter," Uncle Jorge said, "and taped
the ring to the bottom."

"And then you gave it to Mr. Vaslov's brother?" Mom asked.

"*Sí*." Uncle Jorge pulled his hair. "When I rang the doorbell, I handed over the wrong letter."

"Mom's going to be so disappointed." Juanita sniffled.

"What?" Uncle Jorge asked. "Angela knows? How?"

"She was hoping," Juanita explained. "You made such a big deal about meeting at Rockefeller Center tonight under the Christmas tree."

"It's where we went on our first date," Uncle Jorge said.

"I know," Juanita answered. "Romantic."

"Not without the ring!" Uncle Jorge moaned.

"We can talk to Mr. Vaslov's brother!" I touched my Zapato Power wristband. "We can get it back!"

"I hope so!" Uncle Jorge said. "That's why I called you!"

We thought it would be faster to go on a city bus. But the traffic crawled. Police officers were in the streets, waving their arms and blowing whistles.

"Let's get out," Juanita said. "At least we'll move on the sidewalk."

I wanted to say that my Zapato Power could get me there in no time. Except I didn't know where I was going. This wasn't Starwood Park. I needed Juanita to help me find the address.

"How much farther?" Mom asked.

"Look at the signs," Juanita explained. "The last cross street was 39th. This is 38th. Just keep counting till you get to where you want."

So that was the secret to getting around New York!

By the time we reached the address on the envelope, Mom was pooped.

"I hope this building has an elevator," she said.

It didn't. Apartment 6D was six flights up.

"I need to rest." Mom plopped down on the bottom step.

"Let me go ahead," I said. "I can do the stairs in a flash."

"You don't know Mr. Vaslov's brother," Mom worried.

"But I know Mr. Vaslov," I argued. "His brother must be nice too."

Mom took the letter out of her purse. "This envelope has papers to help Mr. Vaslov's family get a green card."

Mr. Vaslov's brother didn't want Uncle Jorge's diamond ring. He wanted to stay in the United States. It was time to make a trade.

"Please, Mom? I'll be quick."

She gave me the letter. "Okay, Freddie. Juanita and I will stay here."

# ZOOM! ZOOM! ZAPATO!

In a blink, I was outside Apartment 6D. A man and a woman were talking inside. I rubbed the buttons on my Zapato Power wristband so I could listen through the door.

"We've waited all day for the man with the colorful hat," a woman said. "He didn't come back for his diamond ring."

"And the green card papers didn't come from my brother," a man's voice said.

"He promised they would be delivered today," the woman said. "What are we going to do?"

"Don't worry!" I knocked on the door. "I have what you need. I'm a friend of Mr. Vaslov's."

"Who is that?" the man asked. "And how does he know what we need?"

For a minute, I thought I was going to have to admit that I

had super hearing. But when Mr.
Vaslov's brother opened the door,
he was so happy to get his green
card papers he didn't care how I
knew so much. He let me explain
Uncle Jorge's mistake.

"Here!" he said. "Take the
love letter and the
diamond back to
your uncle."

Now everybody had what they wanted. Almost!

**ZOOM! ZOOM! ZaPaTO!**

I ran down the stairs to Mom and Juanita.

"Come on!" I waved Uncle Jorge's letter.

A bus came by and we got on. But there were still police officers with whistles and orange cone barriers everywhere.

"Somebody important must be in town." Juanita pointed out the window at black limousines with flags.

"It looks like a motorcade," Mom said.

"Oh no!" Juanita cried. "Mom's going to be waiting under the Christmas tree, thinking Jorge forgot about her."

# 8. The President

We got out of the bus again to walk. The streets were mobbed. People were holding up cameras and cell phones to take pictures.

"What's going on?" Juanita asked the man beside her.

"The president is in town," the man said. "Everyone wants to see."

That included me. The

president of the United States!
*¡Fabuloso!* Only I was too short
to see over the tall grown-ups. I
needed my super bounce. Did I
still have it?

I held my breath and pressed
the second button on my
wristband, the one that used to
give me super bounce.

**BOING! BOING! BOING!**

It worked! I jumped above the
crowd in a swirl of smoke.

**BOING! BOING! BOING!**

The motorcade stopped and
a man in a blue suit opened the
door of the middle limousine.

Out came someone I recognized from pictures and TV. Everybody cheered and waved.

**BOING! BOING! BOING!**

I could have jumped ten feet *without* Zapato Power. This was better than a parade! I couldn't wait to tell Gio back at Starwood Park.

But first I had to bounce down to Mom and Juanita before they realized I was missing.

"Freddie?" Mom asked. "Did you see?"

"Sure did! The president of our country!"

The crowds thinned and we were able to walk faster.

Mom's phone rang.

"Yes!" she answered. "Freddie has the diamond!"

"ANGELA IS WAITING FOR ME!" I didn't need  Zapato Power to hear Uncle Jorge shouting through Mom's phone.

I looked at the street signs and counted. There were only two blocks left to Rockefeller Center. I knew I could get there in less than a blink. The problem was getting away from Mom. Maybe my almost-cousin could help.

"Could you keep my mom busy?" I whispered to Juanita. "So I can run ahead?"

She winked at me. "Good idea, Freddie. You're faster than the rest of us."

Juanita dropped her purse. Keys, combs, pens, and other stuff fell out. Mom stooped to help. I was off.

## ZOOM! ZOOM! ZAPATO!

Getting to the Christmas tree was easy. Finding Angela and Uncle Jorge was not. There were so many people—all there to see the beautiful tree with the millions of colored lights. Luckily, I had my super bounce.

**BOING! BOING! BOING!**

Angela was standing off to the side, looking lonely. But where was Uncle Jorge?

**BOING! BOING! BOING!**

Finally, I spotted a brightly colored hat with a rooster top. It was Uncle Jorge pacing by a bench. I ran over to him.

# ZOOM! ZOOM! Zapato!

"Here!" I handed him the letter. "Go talk to Angela!"

## ZOOM! ZOOM! Zapato!

I got back to Mom before she was finished helping Juanita with her purse.

"Hurry up!" I pulled on her arm.

When we reached the Christmas tree, Uncle Jorge was on one knee, his rooster hat in his hands, watching Angela read her special letter. I rubbed the buttons on

my wristband so I could hear
Angela's answer.

"¡Sí! ¡Sí! ¡Claro!" She nodded
as Uncle Jorge put the ring on her
finger.

"Good work, cousin." Juanita
patted my shoulder.

Mom clapped her hands and

jumped around. She was so happy
she didn't notice Uncle Jorge had
the letter and the ring before we
got there.

The next day Uncle Jorge took
us to the Statue of Liberty, Central
Park, and the Brooklyn Bridge.

I had a lot to tell Claude the
Second when I came home to
Starwood Park. My guinea pig had
been just fine with Gio and Maria.
There were no poop presents on
the carpet.

But I had presents for my friends.

"Thanks, Freddie!" Gio paraded
up and down the sidewalk in his

Statue of Liberty hat. Maria wore
her NYC T-shirt all day.

I gave Mr. Vaslov a tiny model of
the Empire State Building. He put
it on a shelf in his toolshed beside
my too-small zapatos. I was glad to
see them there and not on someone
else's feet.

"What are you going to do with my old shoes?" I asked Mr. Vaslov.

"I'm not sure," he said, rubbing his chin. "What do you think I should do?"

If someone smaller at Starwood Park got super zapatos, they would need help learning how to use them.

"Do you think you could be a good teacher, Freddie?"

That was a good question.

"Maybe." I smiled.

# Don't Miss Freddie's Other Adventures!

HC 978-0-8075-9480-3
PB 978-0-8075-9479-7

PB 978-0-8075-9483-4

HC 978-0-8075-9482-7
PB 978-0-8075-9484-1

HC 978-0-8075-9485-8
PB 978-0-8075-9486-5

HC 978-0-8075-9487-2
PB 978-0-8075-9496-4

HC 978-0-8075-9500-8
PB 978-0-8075-9542-8

HC 978-0-8075-9539-8

**Jacqueline Jules** is the author of forty books, including *Freddie Ramos Takes Off*, a Cybils Award winner. She lives in northern Virginia, just outside Washington, DC. Visit her at www.jacquelinejules.com.

**Miguel Benítez** likes to describe himself as a "part-time daydreamer and a full-time doodler." He lives with his wife and two children in England.